Happy Cat

The Princess and the Unicorn

The king is ill and only the magic
of a unicorn can save him.
But no one believes in unicorns any
more. Except for Princess Lily.
So it's up to her to find one.
But can Lily find a magical unicorn
in time to save the king?

Happy Cat First Readers

The Princess and the Unicorn

Wendy
Blaxland

Illustrated by
Kerry Millard

HAPPY CAT BOOKS

Published by
Happy Cat Books
An imprint of Catnip Publishing Ltd
Islington Business Centre
3-5 Islington High Street
London N1 9LQ

First published by Penguin Books, Australia, 2005

This edition first published 2006
3 5 7 9 10 8 6 4 2

A CIP catalogue record for this book is available
from the British Library

ISBN 978-1-905117-20-8

Printed in Poland

www.catnippublishing.co.uk

To my father. *W.B.*

For my clown. *K.M.*

Chapter One

Once upon a time, there
was a princess called Lily.
Her favourite animal was
the unicorn. Lily dreamed
of seeing a unicorn, of
stroking its curly horn and
watching its gleaming tail
lift in the wind.

Her father, the king, gave Lily a tired smile. 'There are no unicorns any more,' he said.

'Unicorns would be fun to chase,' said her elder brother, Harold, who spent most of his time hunting.

'Unicorns are just stories,' said her other brother, Gerald, who spent most of his time reading.

'You've got candle wax in

your hair again, Gerald,'
said Lily. 'And I'll bet a
unicorn would chase *you*,
Harold.'

Then, one autumn day, the
king fell ill. No one knew
what was wrong.

'Father, do get up,' said
Harold. 'Who's going to run
the kingdom? All those
papers to sign!'

'I'm too tired,' said the

king, from under his white

satin quilt.

'Harold, can't you see he's

sick?' said Lily.

So the papers went

unsigned, and the
merchants went unpaid,
and the people began
to grumble.

The palace doctors shook
their heads. It wasn't the
royal belly, they said, and
the regal forehead wasn't

7

hot. Maybe it was his heart or his soul that was sick.

'Go away,' said the king, and he pulled the white silk sheets over his head.

Chapter Two

The next day, the chief
minister offered twenty
gold coins to anyone who
could cure the king. Soon
half the people in the
kingdom were queuing to
try their luck. It took weeks
for them all to try their

cures, and no one was left

to work in the fields.

Eventually, rain ruined the

wheat crop and a plague of

mice began to eat what
was left.

'Next,' called Gerald.

A doctor in pinstriped
robes stepped forward. 'My
miracle mixture has cured
millions,' he announced.
'Just plaster it on the royal
bald patch.'

'Tried it,' said Harold.
'Didn't work. Next.'

A young woman smiled
nervously. 'My gran said tie

these buttercups under his chin,' she said. 'I'm going to split the reward with her. What's half of twenty?'

But buttercups didn't
cure the king either.

'Enough,' frowned the
chief minister. 'My mother
always gave me prunes in
castor oil when I wouldn't
get out of bed.'

But the king just put
his hands over
his face.

The next morning, an old woman dressed in black limped forward. 'I know what the king needs,' she said.

'Her shawl is tatty,' Harold whispered to Gerald. 'Look at her hairy chin.'

'She smells,' said Gerald, wrinkling his nose.

'Sorry, Gerald, was that your toe?' said Lily. 'This way, Grandmother.'

15

'The only thing that might cure the king,' said the old woman, 'is a unicorn.'

The king turned over and sat up for the first time in three days. 'You're one of the wise women,' he said. 'But I banished all the wise women from the kingdom.'

'Yes, years ago,' said the old woman. 'When this one was born,' she nodded at

Lily, 'and the queen died. You blamed us, though we didn't cause her death. We just couldn't help her.'

'I still miss her,' said
the king. 'I want to be
with her.'

'What about your

kingdom?' asked the
old woman.

'I'm too tired to care
about it,' said the king.

'What your kingdom
needs is a unicorn to restore
it,' said the old woman. 'To
bring the old magic back
to the land.'

'And to make my father
better?' asked Lily.

'Perhaps,' said the old
woman. 'If he really wants
to be.'

'Oh, yes,' said Lily.
'Where can we find a
unicorn?'

'In the land beyond the
sunset,' she said. 'But only
the bravest and most loving
can bring one back. And
only those who believe in
them can find them.'

'If my kingdom needs a unicorn,' said the king, 'then whoever brings me a unicorn will be the new ruler.'

Harold puffed out his chest. 'I'm the eldest, and the bravest. I'll go tomorrow,' he said. 'And I'll be back with a unicorn the very next day.'

Chapter Three

So, the next morning,
Harold set out on his big
black horse through the
forest towards the land
beyond the sunset.

After a week he was still
not back, and the king was
getting worse.

'I've read everything about unicorns,' said Gerald, 'even though they don't exist. I'll go tomorrow, and I'll be back with a unicorn the very next day.'

So, the next morning,

Gerald set out on his big
white horse through the
forest towards the land
beyond the sunset. The
first few snowflakes were
swirling down.

After a week he was still

not back, and the king's eyes were more sunken than ever. Lily stood up from his bedside. 'I'll go,' she said.

'You can't go,' said her father. 'You're a girl.'

'Girls can be brave,' said Lily. 'And I believe in unicorns.'

Her father had nothing more to say for a moment. Then he sat up in bed.

'You'd better take this,'
he said, and reached under
his pillow. He opened up
a crimson silk wrapping,
brought out a dried white

rose, and kissed it. 'Your
mother gave me this,' he
said. 'You'll know when to
use it. I believed in
unicorns once myself.'
And he lay back and closed
his eyes.

So, the next morning, Lily kissed her father goodbye. 'I'll be back as soon as I can,' she said.

Then she wrapped herself up tightly and set out on foot through the forest towards the land beyond the sunset.

Chapter Four

Lily hadn't gone far before
she saw an old woman by
the side of the road.

'Greetings, Grandmother,'
said Lily. 'Is this the way
to the land beyond the
sunset?'

'It is,' said the old woman.

'And have you seen my
brothers riding this way?'
Lily asked.

'Do you mean the fellow

in green on the big black
horse that shouts, "Out of
the way!"? And the chap in
mauve on the big white
horse, with his nose in a

book, who nearly rides folk down?' said the old woman.

'Oh dear,' said Lily. 'Yes, they're my brothers. I'm sorry they were so rude. Would you like one of my wheat cakes?'

'Thank you,' said the old woman. 'Take this in exchange.' And she gave Lily a white rope, fine as cobwebs, folded up into a walnut shell.

'You will know when to use it,' said the old woman.

'Thank you, Grandmother,' said Lily, and she slipped the walnut

safely into her unicorn-
shaped purse.

Later that frozen
afternoon, as Lily walked,
she heard growling. Ahead

of her she saw a white bear by the roadside.

Lily's heart flip-flopped, but she noticed the bear was licking a front paw. So she took a deep breath, and went up to it. 'Good afternoon, Bear,' she said very politely indeed, in case the bear was ready to eat a princess for afternoon tea. 'What's wrong with your paw?'

'A hunter in green
camped here two weeks
ago. He left a trap,' said the
bear, holding up his paw.

Lily saw a cruel wire
buried in the swollen flesh.

'Last week another man rode by on a white horse. But he looked straight through me and said, "There are no bears in this forest." Then he rode away very fast.'

'Oh dear,' said Lily. 'You've met my brothers too. Show me your paw.'

Her embroidery scissors weren't strong enough, so Lily took out the pocket

knife Harold had given her.
'Be brave,' she said to the
bear, and cut the wire.

The bear roared with

pain and Lily closed her
eyes tight so she wouldn't
see herself being eaten.

'That's better,' said the

bear, and Lily opened

one eye.

The bear winked back.

'Now, take three hairs from

my neck fur,' he said. 'You'll know when to use them.'

Lily bound up the bear's paw, and put the three hairs safely in her pocket. Then she went on walking west.

But when the bitter orange sun went down, the sunset was as far away as ever.

'I'll never get there,' she thought. 'And I'm so tired.'

As she spoke, she felt the bear's hairs tickle in her pocket. When she brought them out, they rippled and

grew into a wonderful
white bearskin, just right
to warm a cold princess.

'I wish I was in the land
beyond the sunset,' she said
sleepily. Then she snuggled
into the bearskin and
closed her eyes. She didn't
even feel herself start
to rise.

Chapter Five

The next morning, Lily
awoke in a different land.
The grass was short and
green as velvet. It was
embroidered with strange
flowers, and everything
sparkled with dew.

'This is magical,'

whispered Lily. 'I must be in the land beyond the sunset.' She leapt up, and there, right in front of her, was a unicorn! Its curved flanks gleamed, its long silvery mane rippled with light and yes, its spiral horn shone as if it was made of pure silver.

'Will you come with me to save my father?' asked Lily.

But the unicorn just

looked at her with its great
soft eyes.

Suddenly, Lily felt the
dried white rose in her
pocket flutter and swell. As

47

she took it out, she saw
that the rose was fresh
again. She held it out on
her hand to the unicorn.
The unicorn sniffed it

deeply, and then lowered its
head to Lily. She opened
her walnut shell, and took
out the white silk rope, and
slipped it over
the unicorn's

head. Then she led the
unicorn down to the sea.

There the walnut shell
grew big enough to be
a boat, and Lily led the
unicorn aboard. Back
over the sea of sleep she
journeyed, her head
pillowed on the unicorn's
soft round side.

The next morning, Lily led
the unicorn back through

the forest until she saw her
father's castle.

There, on the edge of the
wintry forest, she saw her

brother, Harold. His green
clothes were ragged, as if
he had slept rough. His
black horse was thin and
its coat was scruffy.

When he saw Lily, he
shouted to her, 'Good girl!
Step to one side, and I'll
shoot the beast!' And he
unslung his bow and fitted
an arrow.

'No!' cried Lily. 'Don't you
dare!' She flung her arms

round the unicorn's neck
until her brother lowered
his bow.

Then, from behind the
snowdrifts limped a white

53

horse, with its head drooping. Gerald, sitting cross-legged on its back, snapped his book shut.

'Well done, Lily,' he called. 'I'll take it from you now. I know all about unicorns.'

And he rode close, but the unicorn flashed its eyes at him and snorted.

The two brothers drew back.

'Perhaps you'd better lead it in yourself,' suggested Harold.

And Lily did.

Chapter Six

The unicorn stepped
carefully as if it was used
to palaces, and at every
step the marble floor rang
like a bell. But Lily hardly
noticed. All she could think
about was her father. Her
hands trembled on his

bed-chamber doorknob.

Were they too late?

There lay her father, eyes closed.

'We're back, Father,' said Lily. 'Here's the unicorn.'

Lily held her breath until she saw the corners of her father's mouth curve. When the smile reached her father's eyes, they opened slowly.

'Lily,' he said, 'did you

really find a unicorn?'

'Yes, Father,' she
whispered. 'Look how
he shines.'

'I've always wanted to see a unicorn. Thank you, blossom,' said the king, and he held Lily in a long hug.

'Oh, Father,' she said.

'It's all right, child,' he said, stroking her hair. 'I'm ready to go. You'll make a fine ruler.'

'Leave him now,' said the chief minister.

So Lily led the unicorn to the palace gardens.

As it entered, the snow
melted clean away from the
grave in the middle of the
garden. Leaves sprang fresh
and green around it, and

bluebells pushed their way
up, but Lily was too sad
to smile.

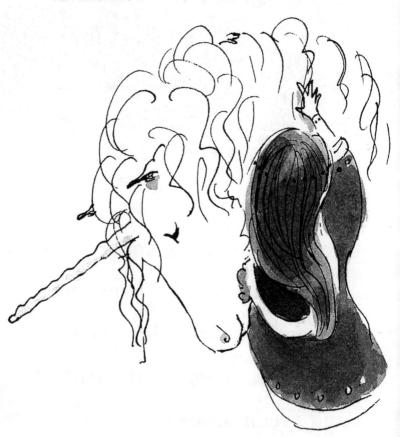

Then she felt the
unicorn's horn nudge her.
Lily flung her arms around
his soft neck and wept into
the mane that smelt of
fresh hay and lavender.

Chapter Seven

When Lily lifted her head, she saw the chief minister in front of her, holding a crimson robe. Harold and Gerald were standing behind him. They all knelt and said, 'Long live the queen.'

Lily looked at the unicorn
standing next to her
mother's grave, and knew
that no one can stop the
turning of the world's

seasons, not even a king's
daughter.

Lily walked with her
brothers to the palace steps

where the people had
gathered. All the bells of
the kingdom were tolling.

Lily stood at the top of

the palace steps and watched as the unicorn kept on walking through the gardens. Wherever its hooves touched, flowers sprang, and the people pointed and whispered. As it reached the edge of the forest, the snow rolled back, and the woods began to flower.

Lily raised her hand.

'Goodbye,' she called.

'Thank you.' She knew the unicorn had heard, before it walked away towards the

land beyond the sunset.

Then Lily turned to her brothers. 'Harold,' she said, 'we need to draw up laws about only hunting animals for food. And look at planting new crops.'

Harold shrugged, and then he nodded. 'You were pretty brave – for a girl,' he added.

'Watch it,' said Lily to her eldest brother, and gave

him a hug. 'You're minister
for lands and forests now.'

'Gerald,' she said to her
other brother, 'I want every
child in the kingdom to be

given a book to mark
this day.'

Gerald smiled. 'What

about *The History of Unicorns*?' he said. 'I'm just about ready to write it.'

'Sounds good,' said Lily. 'You're the new minister for education, of course.'

Then she turned to the chief minister. 'The palace garden needs to be replanted,' she said. 'We need lots of roses, in case we ever need to fetch a unicorn again.'

'Of course, your majesty,' he said and bowed.

Lily looked around at the fresh spring flowers sparkling in the sun, and smiled.